HAPPY FEET™

Chillin' with Mumble
The Truth About Penguins

PSS!
PRICE STERN SLOAN

ISBN 0-8431-2102-5   10 9 8 7 6 5 4 3 2 1

Everyone knows those penguins from *Happy Feet* are really cool, especially when they're tap dancing. So maybe penguins can't really tap dance, but a lot of what you saw in the movie is true. Inside this book you'll see scenes from the movie along with information about the real-life penguins that were the inspiration for Mumble, Gloria, Ramon, and the other characters from *Happy Feet*.

This is Mumble. He's a tap-dancing Emperor penguin with a lot of heart!

Table of Contents

Physical Features of Emperor Penguins

Emperor penguins live far, far away—as far south as you can go—on the cold continent of Antarctica.

What are Emperor penguins?

🖤 Emperor penguins have black feathers covering their heads and backs and white feathers down the front of their bodies. Adult Emperor penguins also have yellow markings near their ears.

🖤 Emperor penguins are the largest kind of penguin—they can weigh up to ninety pounds and grow to be three or four feet tall!

🖤 Emperor penguins can live to be up to twenty years old!

Baby Mumble

Memphis

Norma Jean

Baby Gloria

Mumble and his parents, Norma Jean and Memphis, and his friend, Gloria, are all Emperor penguins.

Emperor Penguin Moms and Dads

Every year in March, Emperor penguins walk for weeks and weeks to get to the rookery where they will all gather and find their mates. The rookery is the place that these penguins were born—and their chicks will be born there, too! After the penguins arrive at the rookery, the male arches his back and gives a loud cry that sounds like singing. The female hears that call and comes to him.

Mumble's parents, Memphis and Norma Jean, hear each other's Heartsongs through the crowd.

Norma Jean and Memphis love each other very much.

Once the two penguins have met each other, they sing. They learn each other's voices so well that they can recognize them even when they've been apart for a long time. No penguin has the same song as another. It's what makes each penguin unique.

Emperor Penguin Birth and Growth

After a penguin mother lays her egg, she is very hungry. That's because she has lost about a third of her body weight! She must go back to the ocean to find food. But before she leaves, she gives the egg to the penguin father so he can keep it warm through the harsh winter. He places the egg in his brood pouch, a cozy little spot on the lower belly, just above the penguin's feet.

While the mothers are away, the fathers brave the coldest part of winter. They gather in a huddle to stay warm against the wind—and take turns being on the outside of the circle. That way, all the penguins spend equal time in the middle of the huddle where it's warmer.

Norma Jean gives Memphis their egg to keep safe while she goes to look for food. Then the two lovebirds say good-bye to each other.

Memphis and Mumble meet each other for the first time.

Now it is time for the egg to hatch. Out pops a fluffy newborn chick! The mother usually makes it back to the rookery around the time when the egg hatches. When she returns, she feeds her chick right away. The chick reaches inside its mother's beak to get food that she has stored in the back of her throat.

Throughout the rest of the winter and into the spring, the penguin parents take turns going back and forth to the ocean to find food for themselves and their chick. The penguin mothers and fathers also sing to their baby so that it can recognize them when they get back!

Super Swimmers

Penguins don't go into the ocean until they lose their baby down and grow adult feathers. This happens when they are about four to five months old. But as soon as they dive in, they're expert swimmers. Penguins swim very quickly, and can hold their breath underwater for three minutes at a time. There have even been some penguins who can hold their breath for up to twenty minutes!

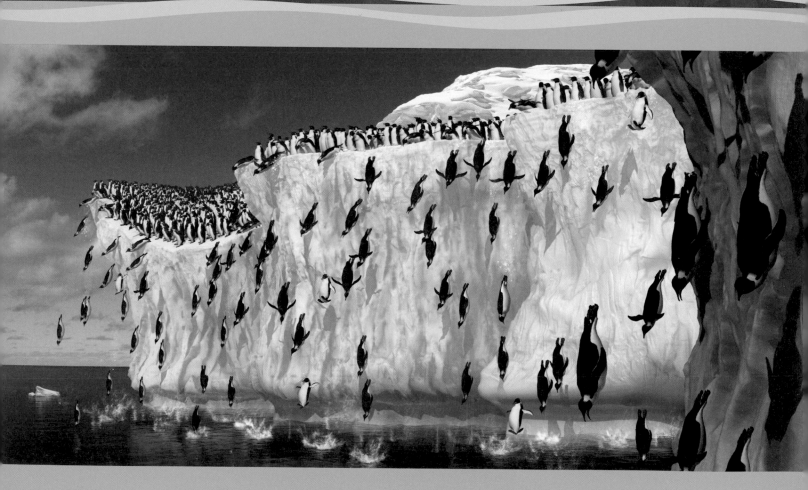

The Emperor Land penguin graduates dive into the sea for the first time.

Tap - Tap - Tippity - Tap - Tap-Tap - Tippity - Tap - Rap -a-tap

HAPPY FEET™

Accidentally Cool

© WBEI (s06)

© WBEI (s06)

© WBEI (s06)

Sing to this.

© WBEI (s06)

© WBEI (s06)

© WBEI (s06)

Gloria and Mumble swim together.

Because penguins are white on the front and black on the back, some people think they look like they're wearing tuxedos. But there's a reason for the way they look—it camouflages them from predators! When penguins swim, it is hard to see their black backs through the dark water from above. And from below, their white bellies blend right into the sunlight coming through the water!

Other Types of Penguins

Emperor penguins aren't the only kind of penguins in the world. There are sixteen other species, including Adelie penguins. Like Emperor penguins, Adelie penguins also live in Antarctica.

What are Adelie penguins?

- Adelie penguins are pretty small. The average Adelie penguin is only two feet tall.

- These penguins live in big colonies, and they're very noisy.

- Unlike Emperor penguins, Adelie penguins do not sing to meet mates. Instead, male Adelies give pebbles to female Adelies as presents. Then they use the pebbles to build nests!

Meet Nestor, Lombardo, Rinaldo, Raul, and Ramon.
They're five great *amigos* who really look up to Mumble!

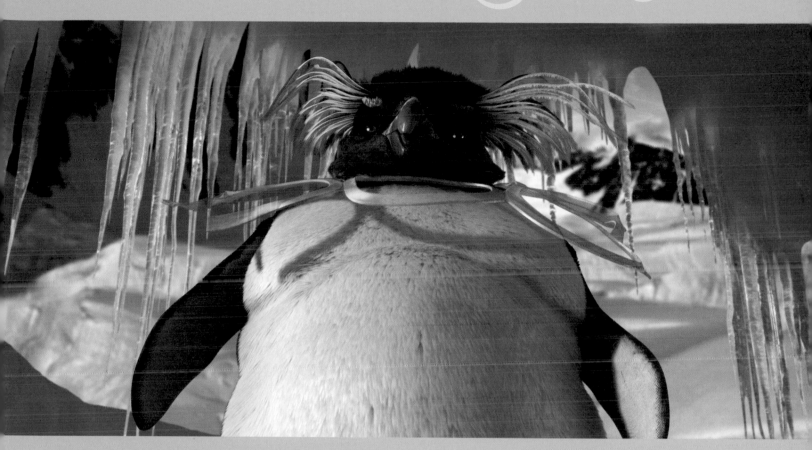

Lovelace is a very famous Rockhopper penguin. He says the plastic around his neck is a talisman bestowed upon him by the Mystic Beings.

Rockhopper penguins don't live in Antarctica but very close to it. What are Rockhopper penguins?

- Like Adelie penguins, Rockhopper penguins are usually about two feet tall.

- Rockhopper penguins have yellow and orange crests of feathers on their heads.

- Rockhopper penguins don't waddle like other penguins. Instead they hop from one place to another!

Penguin Predators

Whether they're on land or in the water, Emperor penguins need to be careful of predators. Brown skua birds are the chief predators of penguin chicks. And when they're in the water, penguins always need to be careful of Leopard seals and orca whales.

Mumble races away from a very unfriendly Leopard seal.

Penguin Prey

Penguins have their own prey, too. They eat underwater animals like fish, squid, and krill. (Krill are tiny animals that look like shrimp.) And although penguins always swim in big groups, they each catch their own food.

Mumble gives Gloria a fish.

An Endangered Habitat

The food supply for Antarctic penguins is getting smaller every day. Too much fishing by humans in the Antarctic has made it harder and harder for penguins to find food.

Mumble, Lovelace, and the Amigos make it to the Forbidden Shore and see fishing ships in the water.

Mumble sees the nets filled with fish. "Stop! You're taking all our fish," he yells.

Penguins are also being harmed by pollution. Burning fuels like coal, oil, and gas causes the earth's temperature to rise. That makes the ice melt—and without ice, there would be nowhere for the penguins to live. Penguins are also threatened by trash and chemicals that drift into the waters around their home.

What Can You Do to Help the Penguins?

- When you throw away plastic six-pack can rings, make sure to snip the rings apart so penguins like Lovelace don't get caught in them.

- Plant trees. They help keep the Earth cool.

- Reduce, reuse, and recycle! Reduce by using only what you need. Reuse products like paper by writing on both sides. Recycle paper, aluminum cans, and glass!

- Always turn off the lights and television when you leave a room. Using electricity burns a lot of fuel.

- Walk or ride your bike short distances instead of riding in a car. Cars create air pollution. You can also encourage your parents to carpool and to use public transportation.

- Ask the government to help the penguins. You can write to your local congressperson to let him or her know about your concern. Ask your parents how to get in touch!

- Spread the word. Tell your friends what you've learned about helping penguins just like Mumble, Gloria, Ramon, and friends!

Now you know the truth about penguins!

Mumble and the rest of the penguins dance for joy—Emperor Land is saved!